Dear Parents:

Congratulations! Your child is taking the first steps on an exciting journey. The destination? Independent reading!

STEP INTO READING® will help your child get there. The program offers five steps to reading success. Each step includes fun stories and colorful art or photographs. In addition to original fiction and books with favorite characters, there are Step into Reading Non-Fiction Readers, Phonics Readers and Boxed Sets, Sticker Readers, and Comic Readers—a complete literacy program with something to interest every child.

Learning to Read, Step by Step!

Ready to Read   Preschool–Kindergarten
• big type and easy words • rhyme and rhythm • picture clues
For children who know the alphabet and are eager to begin reading.

Reading with Help   Preschool–Grade 1
• basic vocabulary • short sentences • simple stories
For children who recognize familiar words and sound out new words with help.

Reading on Your Own   Grades 1–3
• engaging characters • easy-to-follow plots • popular topics
For children who are ready to read on their own.

Reading Paragraphs   Grades 2–3
• challenging vocabulary • short paragraphs • exciting stories
For newly independent readers who read simple sentences with confidence.

Ready for Chapters   Grades 2–4
• chapters • longer paragraphs • full-color art
For children who want to take the plunge into chapter books but still like colorful pictures.

STEP INTO READING® is designed to give every child a successful reading experience. The grade levels are only guides; children will progress through the steps at their own speed, developing confidence in their reading.

Remember, a lifetime love of reading starts with a single step!

*A special thanks to the wonderful people of
the Pacific Islands for inspiring us on this
journey as we bring the world of* Moana *to life.*

Copyright © 2016 Disney Enterprises, Inc. All rights reserved. Published in the United States
by Random House Children's Books, a division of Penguin Random House LLC, 1745 Broadway,
New York, NY 10019, and in Canada by Penguin Random House Canada Limited, Toronto, in
conjunction with Disney Enterprises, Inc.

Step into Reading, Random House, and the Random House colophon are registered trademarks of
Penguin Random House LLC.

Visit us on the Web!
StepIntoReading.com
randomhousekids.com

Educators and librarians, for a variety of teaching tools, visit us at RHTeachersLibrarians.com

ISBN 978-0-7364-3644-1 (trade) — ISBN 978-0-7364-8225-7 (lib. bdg.) —
ISBN 978-0-7364-3645-8 (ebook)

Printed in the United States of America   20 19 18 17 16 15 14 13 12 11 10

DISNEY MOANA

Moana
Finds the Way

by Susan Amerikaner

illustrated by the Disney Storybook Art Team

Random House 🏠 New York

Te Fiti is an island.

She once gave life to all.

The demigod Maui

stole Te Fiti's heart.

Maui lost the heart.

Darkness spread.

People stopped sailing

on the open ocean.

Moana lives
on an island.
She loves the ocean.

It gives her a shiny gift.

It is the heart of Te Fiti!

Moana grows up.
Gramma Tala shows her
a cave full of boats.
Moana's people once
loved to sail!

Moana thinks she would
love to sail, too.

Gramma Tala tells Moana
she must find Maui
and return Te Fiti's heart.

Moana agrees.

She will sail!

She will wayfind!

Moana does not know
how to sail.
But she loves the ocean.
She tries to sail.

A storm comes.

Moana is lost.

Moana finds Maui.
Maui does not think
Moana can learn
to wayfind.

He does not want
to help.
The ocean makes
him teach her.

Moana must learn
to use the sun.
She must learn
to feel the waves.

Moana works hard.

She uses the stars.

She feels the waves.

She finds the way!

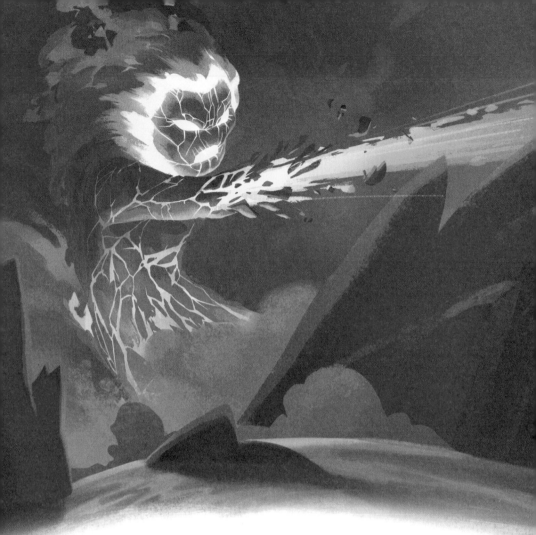

Monster Te Kā comes.

Big waves rock the boat.

Moana sails fast.

She holds on.

Te Kā is strong.

Moana is smart.

She finds a way.

Moana returns

the heart of Te Fiti.

The darkness leaves.

Plants grow.

Te Fiti blooms.

Life returns

to the islands.

Moana finds her way
back home.
Her family is happy
to see her.

Moana leads her people
to new islands.
She is a great
wayfinder.

She is Moana.

Disney

MOANA

Disney

MOANA

Disney

MOANA

Disney

MOANA

The
Kakamora

Pua
and Heihei

© Disney

© Disney

Maui
and Moana

Moana
and
Pua

© Disney

© Disney

Moana

Maui

Pua

Heihei

© Disney

DISNEP
M☉ANA

DISNEP
M☉ANA

DISNEP
M☉ANA

DISNEP
M☉ANA

Heihei

Pua

© Disney

© Disney

Maui

Moana

© Disney

© Disney

Moana and Pua

Maui and Moana

© Disney

© Disney

Pua and Heihei

The Kakamora

© Disney

© Disney

DISNEY
MOANA

DISNEY
MOANA

DISNEY
MOANA

DISNEY
MOANA